The ABC Bag

The ABC Bags
© 1999 Creative Teaching Press, Inc.
Written by Margaret Allen, Ph.D.
Photographed by Michael Jarrett
Project Director: Luella Connelly
Editor: Joel Kupperstein
Art Director: Tom Cochrane

Published in the United States of America by:
Creative Teaching Press, Inc.
P.O. Box 6017
Cypress, CA 90630-0017

CTP 2908

Paste

The ABC Bags

"Let's plan the ABC bags,"
Jeff calls to the kids.

Jeff picks one.
"I got E. I will make an egg."

"You pick one, Russ," says Jeff. Russ gets B.
"I will make a ball," says Russ.

Will picks. "What did you get, Will?" asks Russ.
"I got H," says Will. "I will make a hill."

Nell gets W.
"I will make a well," says Nell.

Tess picks D. "Can I make a doll?" asks Tess.
"Yes, Tess," says Jeff. "Make a doll."

Jeff gets the bags and the pens.

The kids plan.

The kids cut.

But the stuff will not stick.

"Oh, no!" yell the kids. "This is stiff stuff!
It will not stick at all!"

"We can plan and we can cut.
But we can not stick."

"We did not get ABC bags," says Jeff.
"No, Jeff. We did not get ABC bags," say the kids.

14

"We got an ABC mess!"

BOOK 8: The ABC Bags

Focus Skills: double f, l, and s

Focus-Skill Words			Sight Words	Story Words
Jeff	doll	yell	asks	egg
stiff	hill	mess	one	make
stuff	Will	Russ	this	says
all	Nell	Tess	what	
ball	well			
calls	will			

Focus-Skill Words contain a new skill or sound introduced in this book.

Sight Words are among the most common words encountered in the English language (appearing in this book for the first time in the series).

Story Words appear for the first time in this book and are included to add flavor and interest to the story. They may or may not be decodable.

Interactive Reading Idea

Have your young reader make his or her own ABC bags. Label lunch sacks with the letters of your reader's first name, one on each bag, and invite him or her to cut out pictures from magazines or locate real objects to place in the appropriate bags.